# JOURNEY

*Aaron Becker*

WALKER BOOKS
AND SUBSIDIARIES
LONDON • BOSTON • SYDNEY • AUCKLAND

# For Josephine

This book would not have been possible without the help of some great friends and colleagues, notably Joanne Taylor, Laurel Snyder, David Costello, Diane deGroat, Jeff Mack, Linda Pratt, Maryellen Hanley, Mary Lee Donovan and, last but not least, my wife, Darci Palmquist.

First published 2013 by Walker Books Ltd
87 Vauxhall Walk, London SE11 5HJ

10 9 8 7 6 5 4 3 2 1

© 2013 Aaron Becker

British Library Cataloguing in Publication Data: a catalogue record for this book is available from the British Library

ISBN 978-1-4063-4230-7

www.walker.co.uk

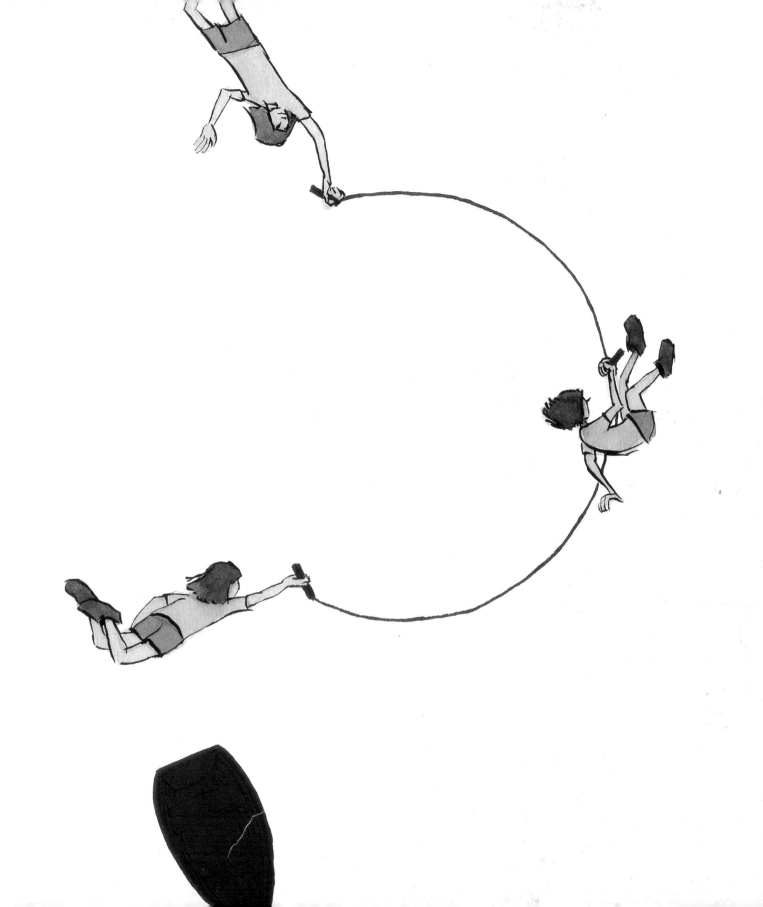

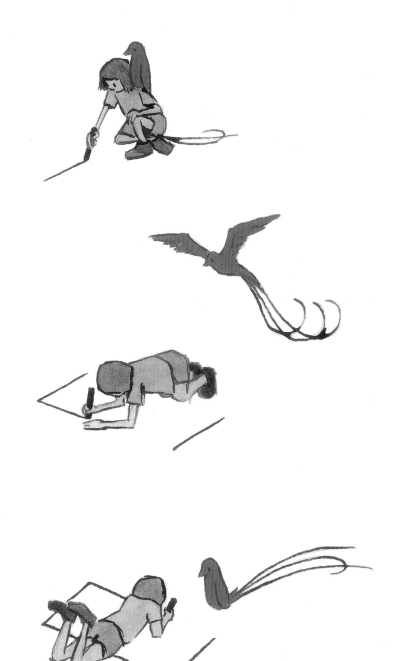